12/8/16

TO CHARLIE

READ ALL THE BOOKS YOU CAN!
ENJOY!

NEW YORK CITY

A TO Z

Kip Cosson

I dedicate my book to the following three amazing people in my life:

To Aunt Avie,
Thank you for always being there for me with your love and encouragement!

To Joe & Dottie,
Thank you for your friendship and love, it has inspired me to live my dreams!

First Edition 2014
Second Printing 2015

Published by Kip Kids of New York
KipKids@aol.com

Text and illustration © 2014
by Kipton P. Cosson

Visit Us At www.KipKids.com

ISBN 978-0-9789384-3-7

Printed in Malaysia

A is for an anteater named José in apartment 4A who loves alphabet soup!
He invites a family of ants above in 5A to join him in a bowl.
They all say, "IN a bowl of soup? No WAY José!"

B is for blueberry bagels being munched by two big blue bears having brunch
A bunch of busy bees buzz around waiting for a table by the window.

C is for the cool cat riding in a yellow taxi to Columbus Circle.
The cab stops at a light as a parade of colorful clowns cross the street.

D is for a super-duper deluxe dump truck with four ducks flying downtown. Danny duck is late and does his best to catch up with the others. The work they do is never done as they dig deep in the dirt.

Danny's Lunch

E is for a stack of eager elephants balanced as high as the Empire State Building. One tickle of a feather and they could all come tumbling down to earth.

Fifi's Fresh Flower Shop

OPEN

F is for Fifi the French fox selling her fresh-cut flowers.
A firefighter stops every Friday to buy five tulips for his family in the Bronx.

G is for the great big George Washington Bridge.
A group of giddy goats take a trip from New Jersey to see Grand Central Station.
Gus the giraffe goes into the city to sell his giant grapes at the Greenmarket.

THE SCHOOL OF GIFTED GOATS

622

H is for the hungry hippo with a heron on his head.
They make a deal—a hamburger for a ride for two along the High Line.
Now everyone is happy!

I is for the **I**nternational **I**nsect Festival on Staten **I**sland!
Colorful creatures fly **i**n from all around the world: **I**ndia, **I**celand, **I**taly...
They feast on **i**vy, **i**rises and **i**mported **i**ce cubes on a stick.

J is for seven jellyfish doing their morning jumping jacks with Ned and Meece. They jiggle and shake their jelly bellies as they jump for joy along Chelsea Piers.

K is for Kayla Lou the kangaroo out shop-hopping around New York.
She stops to buy a Kip Kids tee shirt from the local artist.

L is for a line of six ladybugs walking branch by branch down Lexington Avenue. Suddenly it begins to rain, so they quickly put on their little leaf umbrella hats. One splat on the head by a large raindrop and their antennas could go loopy.

M is for a magical moon over Manhattan.
Two friends count the many millions of stars high above New York.
Meece makes a wish upon a star for a world with more love and more cheese.

N is for New York, New York, a place Ned Penguin loves to visit.
He and Meece always have a big adventure in the city that never sleeps.
This time they will spend the night in the Museum of Natural History with nine friends

O is for one ostrich wearing orange at the opera on opening night.
She looks all around as the orchestra plays down below.
Oh how wonderful it is to see a sold-out performance of *Otello*!

P is for a pepperoni-pizza party for eight peppy penguins in Prospect Park.
They play their favorite game, pin the tail on the pink pig.

Q is for three quirky quails living in a quaint area of Queens.
Quietly they rest outside...but should Mr. Cat come along, they will quickly fly away!

R is for the rhinos riding a bicycle-built-for-two in Riverside Park. They race past a raccoon with a stack of red raspberries balanced on his nose.

S is for a street sweeper that slowly swishes through SoHo.
Every Saturday a seal, a sheep, and a skunk stand watching
the big brushes swirl and spin, sucking up the garbage.

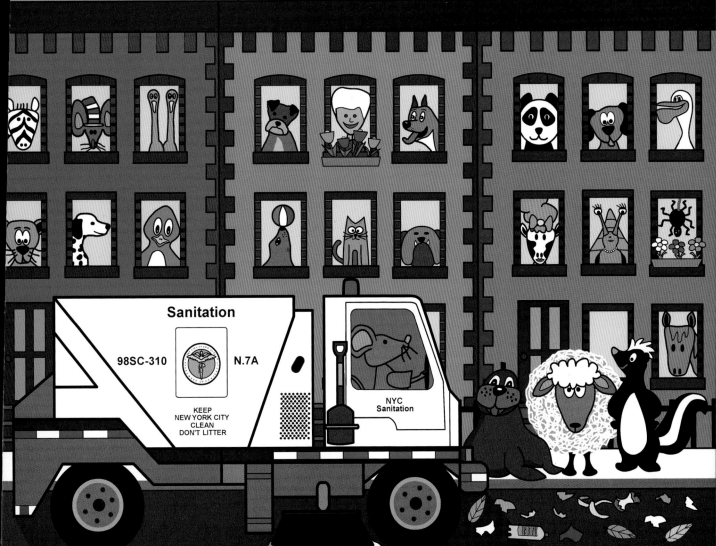

FORECAST: 80% CHANCE OF TURNIP & TOMATO SHOWERS

PENGUINETTES ON BROADWAY

MEECE THE MAGICIAN

BEST MUSICAL!!

MAGIC NIGHT!!

NEW YORK TOUR BUS

T is for the tourists taking a tour bus to the theater in Times Square. Along the way they see purple and red lightning bolts as it starts to thunder. Soon it begins to rain turnips and tomatoes from the sky.

U is for the unicorn mime riding a unicycle in Union Square Park.
He points up towards the sky to a colorful rainbow without uttering a word.

V is for the vampire bats from Vegas on vacation in the Village.
They sleep upside down during the day at the very trendy Velvet Bat Hotel.
In the evening they will wake up and venture out to view the vibrant city life.

Welcome To The Velvet Bat Hotel

W is for Wednesday, the day three friends Waldo, Wendy, and Willow meet for their morning walk around Washington Square Park. They wag and wiggle their tails with woofs of excitement!

X is for Xerus the African squirrel who loves to play the xylophone underwater.
He performs in Brooklyn at the Aquarium for a school of x-ray fish and their friends.

THE YACHT SEA

Y is for a yacht with ten yellow-eyed penguins from New Zealand.
They sail into New York harbor with one seasick penguin.
The boat has been rocked up and down like a yo-yo for over 8,000 miles.

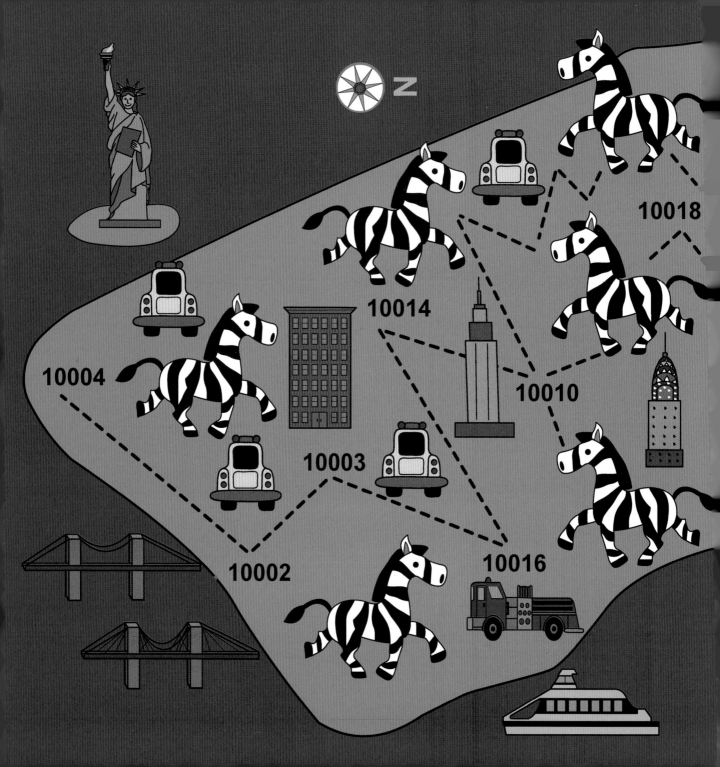

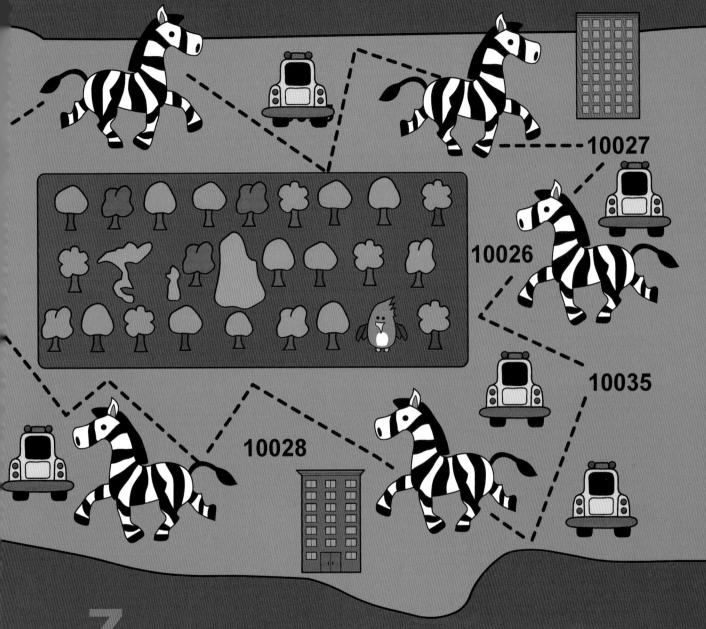

10027

10026

10035

10028

Z is for the zillions of zany zebras that visit New York City.
They love to zigzag from zip code to zip code across Manhattan!

The Alphabet Chart - A to Z

Aa =		**Jj =**		**Ss =**	
Bb =		**Kk =**		**Tt =**	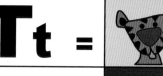
Cc =	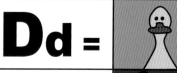	**Ll =**		**Uu =**	
Dd =		**Mm =**		**Vv =**	
Ee =		**Nn =**	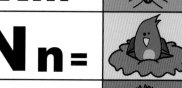	**Ww =**	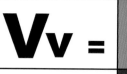
Ff =		**Oo =**	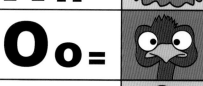	**Xx =**	
Gg =		**Pp =**		**Yy =**	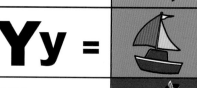
Hh =		**Qq =**		**Zz =**	
Ii =		**Rr =**			

Below is a message from Ned & Meece.

Place a letter in the blank box below that matches the picture.
Use the Alphabet chart on the opposite page to solve the message.

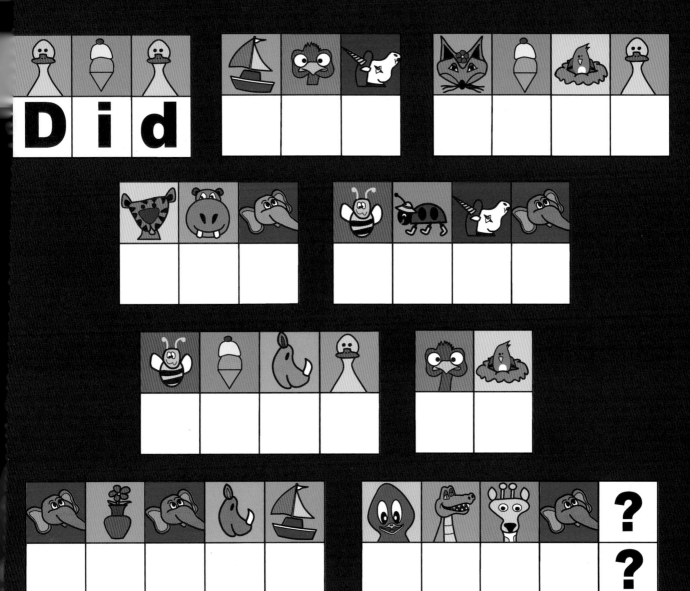

About The Author/Artist

Kip Cosson is an award winning writer and illustrator of children's books. He is a Texan who lives in New York's Greenwich Village. His career began as an artist in 1991 by hand painting his artwork on children's clothing.

Book Awards For New York City A to Z

- Won Best Children's Picture Book at the 2015 New York Book Festival.
- Finalist in the 2015 New Generation Indie Book Awards - Children's Picture Book.
- Finalist in the 2015 International Book Awards - Children's Educational Book.

For more information, Kip can be reached at : KipKids@aol.com

Books By Kip

A wonderful children's guide to NYC. The map and checklist in the back are a great way to learn where everything is located.

Travel to all five boroughs of NYC with Ned & Meece and learn about the importance to always dream big. Remember every vote counts!

This multilingual New York book is in six languages: English, Spanish, German, French, Italian and Japanese.

Visit Kip's website at www.KipKids.com

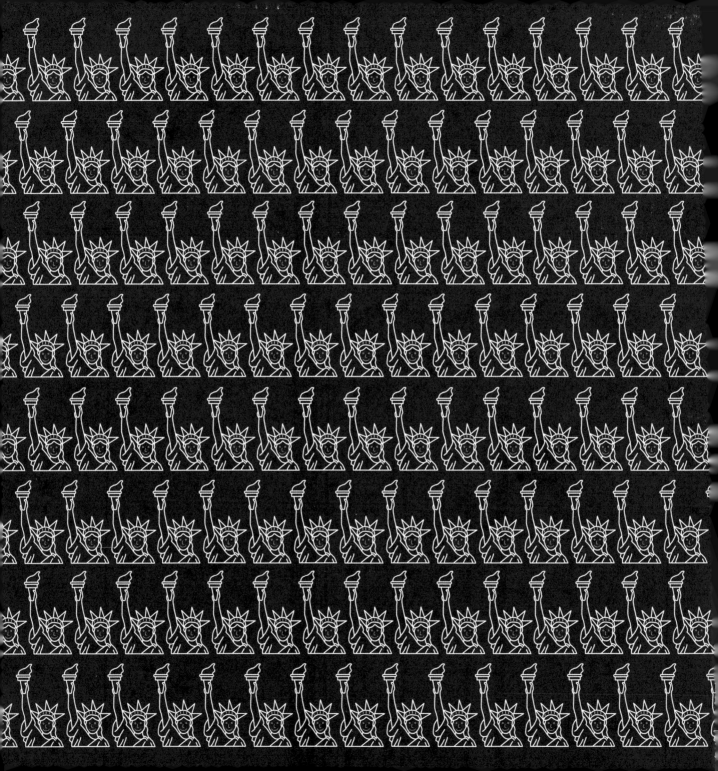

BOOK ONE

Proof of Identity

1

THE social worker was older than she had expected; perhaps the nameless official who arranged these matters thought that graying hair and menopausal plumpness might induce confidence in the adopted adults who came for their compulsory counseling. After all, they must be in need of reassurance of some kind, these displaced persons whose umbilical cord was a court order, or why had they troubled to travel this bureaucratic road to identity? The social worker smiled her encouraging professional smile. She said, holding out her hand, "My name is Naomi Henderson and you're Miss Philippa Rose Palfrey. I'm afraid I have to begin by asking you for some proof of identity."

Philippa nearly replied: "Philippa Rose Palfrey is what I'm called. I'm here to find out who I am," but checked herself in time, sensing that such an affectation would be an unpropitious beginning to the interview. They both knew why she was here. And she wanted the session to be a success; wanted it to go her way without being precisely clear what way that was. She unclipped the fastening of her leather shoulder bag and handed over in silence her passport and the newly acquired driving license.

The attempt at reassuring informality extended to the furnishing of the room. There was an official-looking desk, but Miss Henderson had moved from behind it as soon as Philippa was announced and had motioned her to one of the two vinyl-covered armchairs on each side of a low table. There were even flowers on the table, in a small blue bowl lettered "a present from Polperro." It held a mixed bunch of roses. These weren't the scentless, thornless buds of the florist's window. These were garden roses, recognized from the garden at Caldecote Terrace: Peace, Superstar, Albertine, the blossoms overblown, already peeling with only one or two tightly furled buds, darkening at the lips and destined never to open. Philippa wondered if the social worker had brought them in from her own garden. Perhaps she was retired, living in the country, and had been recruited part-time for this particular job. She could picture her clumping round her rose bed in the brogues and serviceable tweeds she was wearing now, snipping away at roses which were due for culling, might just last out the London day. Someone had watered the flowers overenthusiastically. A milky bead lay like a pearl between two yellow petals and there was a splash on the table top. But the imitation mahogany wouldn't be stained; it wasn't really wood. The roses gave forth a damp sweetness, but they weren't really fresh. In these easy chairs no visitor had ever sat at ease. The smile which invited her confidence and trust across the table was bestowed by courtesy of section twenty-six of the Children Act 1975.

She had taken trouble with her appearance, but then she always did, presenting herself to the world with self-conscious art, daily remaking herself in her own image. The aim this morning had been to suggest that no trouble had in fact been taken, that this interview had induced no special anxiety, warranted no exceptional care. Her strong corn-colored hair, bleached by the summer so that no two strands were exactly the same gold, was drawn back from a high forehead and knotted in a single heavy plait. The wide mouth with its strong, curved upper lip and sensuous droop at each corner was devoid of lipstick, but she had applied her eyeshadow with care, emphasizing her most remarkable feature, the luminous, slightly protuberant green eyes. Her honey-colored skin glistened with sweat. She had lingered too long in the Embankment Gardens,

(7)

unwilling to arrive early, and in the end had had to hurry. She wore sandals and a pale green open-necked cotton shirt above her corduroy trousers. In contrast to this casual informality, the careful ambiguity about money or social class were the possessions which she wore like talismans: the slim gold watch, the three heavy Victorian rings, topaz, cornelian, peridot, the leather Italian bag slung from her left shoulder. The contrast was deliberate. The advantage of remembering virtually nothing before her eighth birthday, the knowledge that she was illegitimate, meant that there was no phalanx of the living dead, no pious ancestor worship, no conditioned reflexes of thought to inhibit the creativity with which she presented herself to the world. What she aimed to achieve was singularity, an impression of intelligence, a look that could be spectacular, even eccentric, but never ordinary.

Her file, clean and new, lay open before Miss Henderson. Across the table Philippa could recognize some of the contents: the orange and brown government information sheet, a copy of which she had obtained from a Citizens Advice Bureau in north London where there had been no risk that she would be known or recognized; her letter to the Registrar General written five weeks ago, the day after her eighteenth birthday, in which she had requested the application form which was the first document to identity; a copy of the form itself. The letter was tagged on top of the file, stark white against the buff of bureaucracy. Miss Henderson fingered it. Something about it, the address, the quality of the heavy linen-based paper apparent even in a copy, evoked, Philippa thought, a transitory unease. Perhaps it was a recognition that her adoptive father was Maurice Palfrey. Given Maurice's indefatigable self-advertisement, the stream of sociological publications which flowed from his department, it would be odd if a senior social worker hadn't heard of him. She wondered whether Miss Henderson had read his *Theory and Technique in Counseling: A Guide for Practitioners*, and if so, how much she had been helped in bolstering her clients' self-esteem—and what a significant word "client" was in social-work jargon—by Maurice's lucid exploration of the difference between developmental counseling and Gestalt therapy.

Miss Henderson said, "Perhaps I ought to begin by telling you how far I'm able to help you. Some of this you probably already know, but I find it useful to get it straight. The Children Act 1975 made important changes in the law relating to access to birth records. It provides that adopted adults—that is, people who are at least eighteen years old—may if they wish apply to the Registrar General for information which will lead them to the original record of their birth. When you were adopted you were given a new birth certificate, and the information which links your present name, Philippa Rose Palfrey, with your original birth certificate is kept by the Registrar General in confidential records. It is this linking information which the law now requires the Registrar General to give you if you want it. The 1975 Act also provides that people adopted before the twelfth of November 1975, that is, before the Act was passed, must attend an interview with a counselor before he or she can be given the information. The reason for this is that Parliament was concerned about making the new arrangements retrospective, since over the years many natural parents gave up their children for adoption and adopters took on the children on the understanding that their natural parentage would remain unknown. So you have come here today so that we can consider together the possible effect of any inquiries you may make about your natural parents, both on yourself and on other people, and so that the information you are now seeking, and to which you have, of course, a legal right, is provided in a helpful and appropriate manner. At the end of our talk, and if you still want it, I shall be able to give you your original name; the name of your natural mother; possibly—but not certainly—the name of your natural father, and the name of the court where your adoption order was made. I shall also be able to give you an application form which you can use to apply to the Registrar General for a copy of your original birth certificate."

She had said it all before. It came out a little too pat. Philippa said, "And there's a standard charge of two pounds fifty pence for the birth certificate. It seems cheap at the price. I know all that. It's in the orange and brown pamphlet."

"As long as it's quite clear. I wonder if you'd like to tell me when you first decided to ask for your birth record. I see that you applied as soon as you were eighteen. Was this a sudden decision, or had you been thinking about it for some time?"

"I decided when the 1975 Act was going through Parliament. I was fifteen then and taking my O-levels. I don't think I gave it a great deal of thought at the time. I just made up my mind that I'd apply as soon as I was legally able to."

"Have you spoken to your adoptive parents about it?"

"No. We're not exactly a communicative family."

Miss Henderson let that pass for the moment.

"And what exactly did you have in mind? Do you want just to know who your natural parents are, or are you hoping to trace them?"

"I'm hoping to find out who I am. I don't see the point of stopping at two names on a birth certificate. There may not even be two names. I know I'm illegitimate. The search may all come to nothing. I know that my mother is dead so I can't trace her, and I may never find my father. But at least if I can find out who my mother was I may get a lead to him. He may be dead too, but I don't think so. Somehow I'm certain that my father is alive."

Normally she liked her fantasies at least tenuously rooted in reality. Only this one was different, out of time, wildly improbable and yet impossible to relinquish, like an ancient religion whose archaic ceremonies, comfortingly familiar and absurd, somehow witness to an essential truth. She couldn't remember why she had originally set her scene in the nineteenth century, or why, learning so soon that this was nonsense since she had been born in 1960, she had never updated the persistent self-indulgent imaginings. Her mother, a slim figure dressed as a Victorian parlor maid, an upswept glory of golden hair under the goffered cap with its two broderie Anglaise streamers, ghostlike against the tall hedge which surrounded the rose garden. Her father in full evening dress striding like a god across the terrace, down the broad walk, under the spray of the fountains. The sloping lawn, drenched by the mellow light of the last sun, glittering with peacocks. The two shadows merging into one shadow, the dark head bending to the gold.

"My darling, my darling. I can't let you go. Marry me."

"I can't. You know I can't."

It had become a habit to conjure up her favorite scenes in the minutes before she fell asleep. Sleep came in a drift of rose leaves. In the earliest dreams her father had been in uniform, scarlet and gold, his chest beribboned, sword clanking at his side. As she grew older she had edited out these embarrassing embellishments. The soldier, the fearless rider to hounds, had become the aristocrat scholar. But the essential picture remained.

There was a globule of water creeping down the petal of the yellow rose. She watched it, fascinated, willing it not to fall. She had distanced her thoughts from what Miss Henderson had been saying. Now she made an effort to attend. The social worker was asking about her adoptive parents.

"And your mother, what does she do?"

"My adoptive mother cooks."

"You mean she works as a cook?" The social worker modified this as if conscious that it could imply some derogation, and added, "She cooks professionally?"

"She cooks for her husband and her guests and me. And she's a juvenile court magistrate, but I think she only took that on to please my adoptive father. He believes that a woman should have a job outside the home, provided, of course, that it doesn't interfere with his comfort. But cooking is her enthusiasm. She's good enough at it to cook professionally, although I don't think she was ever properly taught except at evening classes. She was my father's secretary before they married. I mean that cooking is her hobby, her interest."

"Well, that's nice for your father and you."

Presumably that hint of encouraging patronage was by now too unconsciously part of her to be easily disciplined. Philippa gazed at the woman stonily, noted it, took strength from it.

"Yes, we're both greedy, my adoptive father and I. We can both eat voraciously without putting on weight."

That, she supposed, implied something of an appetite for life, not indiscriminate, since they were both appreciative of good food; perhaps a reinforcement of their belief that one could indulge without having to pay for indulgence. Greed, unlike sex, involved no commitment except to one's self, no violence except to one's own body. She had always taken comfort from her discernment about food and drink. That, at least, could hardly have been caught from his example. Even Maurice, convinced environmentalist that he was, would hardly claim that a nose for claret could be so easily acquired. Learning to enjoy wine, discovering that she had a palate, had been one more reassuring affirmation of inherited taste. She recalled her seventeenth birthday; the three bottles on the table before them, the labels shrouded. She couldn't recall that Hilda had been with them. Surely she must have been present for a family birthday dinner, but in memory she and Maurice celebrated alone. He had said, "Now tell me which you prefer. Forget the purple prose of the color supplements, I want to know what you think in your own words."

She had tasted them again, holding the wine in her mouth, sipping water between each sampling, since she supposed that this was the proper thing to do, watching his bright, challenging eyes.

"This one."

"Why?"

"I don't know. I just like it best."

But he would expect a more considered judgment than that. She added, "Perhaps because with this one I can't distinguish taste from smell and from the feel of it in the mouth. They aren't separate sensations, it's a trinity of pleasure."

She had chosen the right one. There always was a right answer and a wrong answer. This had been one more test successfully passed, one more notch on the scale of approval. He couldn't entirely reject her, couldn't send her back; she knew that. An adoption order couldn't be revoked. That made it the more important that she should justify his choice of her, that she should give value for money. Hilda, who worked for hours in the kitchen preparing their meals, ate and drank little. She would sit, anxious eyes fixed on them as they shoveled in their food. She gave and they took. It was almost too psychologically neat.

Miss Henderson asked, "Do you resent them for adopting you?"

"No, I'm grateful. I was lucky. I don't think I'd have done well with a poor family."

"Not even if they loved you?"

"I don't see why they should. I'm not particularly lovable."

She hadn't done well with a poor family, of that at least she could be certain. She hadn't done well with any of her foster parents. Some smells: her own excreta, the rotting waste outside a restaurant, a young child bundled into soiled clothes on its mother's lap pressed against her by the lurch of a bus, these could evoke a momentary panic that had nothing to do with disgust. Memory was like a searchlight sweeping over the lost hinterland of the self, illuminating scenes with total clarity, the colors gaudy as a child's comic, edges of objects hard as blocks, scenes which could lie for months unremembered in that black wasteland, not rooted, as were other childish memories, in time and place, not rooted in love.

"Do you love them, your adoptive parents?"

She considered. Love. One of the most used words in the language, the most debased. Heloise and Abelard. Rochester and Jane Eyre. Emma and Mr. Knightly. Anna and Count Vronsky. Even within the narrow connotation of heterosexual love it meant exactly what you wanted it to mean.

"No. And I don't think they love me. But we suit each other on the whole. That's more convenient, I imagine, than living with people that you love but don't suit."

"I can see that it could be. How much were you told about the circumstances of your adoption? About your natural parents?"

"As much, I think, as my adoptive mother could tell me. Maurice never talks about it. My adoptive father's a university lecturer, a sociologist. Maurice Palfrey, the sociologist who can write English. His first wife and their son died in a car crash when the boy was three. She was driving. He married my adoptive mother nine months afterward. They discovered that she couldn't have children, so they found me. I was being fostered at the time, so they took over the care of me and after six months applied to the county court and got an adoption order. It was a private arrangement, the kind of thing your new Act would make illegal. I can't think why. It seems to me a perfectly sensible way of going about it. I've certainly nothing to complain of."

"It worked very well for thousands of children and their adopters, but it had its dangers. We wouldn't want to go back to the days when unwanted babies lay in rows of cots in nurseries so that adoptive parents could just go and pick out the one they fancied."

"I don't see why not. That seems to me the only sensible way, as long as the children are too young to know what's happening. That's how you'd pick a puppy or a kitten. I imagine that you need to take to a baby,

(14)

to feel that this is a child that you want to rear, could grow to love. If I needed to adopt, and I never would, the last thing I'd want would be a child selected for me by a social worker. If we didn't take to each other I wouldn't be able to hand it back without the social services department striking me off the books as being one of those neurotic self-indulgent women who want a child for their own satisfaction. And what other possible reason could there be for wanting an adopted child?"

"Perhaps to give that child a better chance."

"Don't you mean, to have the personal satisfaction of giving that child a better chance? It amounts to the same thing."

She wouldn't bother to refute that heresy, of course. Social-work theory didn't err. After all, its practitioners were the new priesthood, the ministry of unbelievers. She merely smiled and persevered, "Did they tell you anything about your background?"

"Only that I'm illegitimate. My adoptive father's first wife came from the aristocracy, an earl's daughter, and was brought up in a Palladian mansion in Wiltshire. I believe that my mother was one of the maids there, who got herself pregnant. She died soon after I was born and no one knew who my father was. Obviously he wasn't a fellow servant; she couldn't have kept that particular secret from the servants' hall. I think he must have been a visitor to the house. There are only two things I can remember clearly about my life before I was eight; one is the rose garden at Pennington, the other is the library. I think that my father, my real father, was there with me. It's possible that one of the upper servants at Pennington put my adoptive father in touch with me after his first wife died. He never speaks about it. I only learned as much as that from my adoptive mother. I suppose Maurice thought that I'd do because I was a girl. He wouldn't want a boy to bear his name unless he were really his son. It would be terribly important to him to know that a son was really his own."

"That's understandable, isn't it?"

"Of course. That's why I'm here. It's important for me to know that my parents really were my own."

"Well, let's say that you think it important."

Her eyes dropped to the file. There was a rustle of papers.

"So you were adopted on the seventh of January 1969. You must have been eight. That's quite old."

"I suppose they thought it was better than taking a very young baby and having broken nights. And my adoptive father could see that I was all right, physically all right, that I wasn't stupid. There wasn't the same risk as with a young baby. I know that there are stringent medical examinations, but one can never be quite sure, not about intelligence, anyway. He couldn't have borne to find himself saddled with a stupid child."

"Is that what he told you?"

"No, it's what I've thought out for myself."

One fact she could be sure of: that she came from Pennington. There was a childhood memory more clear even than that of the rose garden: the Wren library. She knew that she had once stood there under that exuberant seventeenth-century stuccoed ceiling with its garlands and cherubs, had stared down that vast room at the Grinling Gibbons carvings richly spilling from the shelves, at the Roubiliac busts set above the bookcases, Homer, Dante, Shakespeare, Milton. In memory she saw herself standing at the great chart table reading from a book. The book had been almost too heavy to hold. She could still recall the ache in her wrists and the fear that she might drop it. And she was certain that her real father had been with her; that she had been reading aloud to him. She was so sure that she belonged at Pennington that sometimes she was tempted to believe that the earl had been her father. But the fantasy was unacceptable and she rejected it, faithful to the original vision of the visiting aristocrat. The earl must have known if he had fathered a child on one of his servants, and surely, surely he wouldn't have rejected her totally, left her unsought

(16)

and unrecognized for eighteen years. She had never been back to the house, and now that the Arabs had bought it and it had become a Moslem fortress she never would. But when she was twelve she had searched in Westminster reference library for a book on Pennington and had read a description of the library. There had been a picture too. The confirmation had jolted her heart. It was all there, the plaster ceiling, the Grinling Gibbons carvings, the busts. But her memory had come first. The child standing beside the chart table holding the book in her aching hands must have existed.

She scarcely heard the rest of the counseling. If it had to be done, she supposed that Miss Henderson was making a good enough job of it. But it was no more than a statutory nuisance, the way in which uneasy legislators had salved their consciences. None of the arguments so conscientiously put forward could shake her resolve to track down her father. And how could their meeting, however delayed, be unwelcome to him? She wouldn't be coming empty-handed. She had her Cambridge scholarship to lay at his feet.

She said, wrenching her mind back to the present, "I can't see the point of this compulsory counseling. Are you supposed to dissuade me from tracing my father? Either our legislators think I have a right to know, or they don't. To give me the right and at the same time officially try to discourage me from exercising it seems muddled thinking even for Parliament. Or do they just have a bad conscience about retrospective legislation?"

"Parliament wants adopted people to think carefully about the implications of what they're doing, what it could mean for themselves, for their adoptive parents, for their natural parents."

"I have thought. My mother is dead, so it can't hurt her. I don't propose to embarrass my father. I want to know who he is, or was, if he's dead. That's all. If he's still alive, I should like to meet him, but I'm not thinking of bursting in on a family party and announcing that I'm his bastard. And I don't see how any of this concerns my adoptive parents."

"Wouldn't it be wise, and kinder, to discuss it first with your adoptive parents?"

"What is there to discuss? The law gives me a right. I'm exercising it."

Thinking back on the counseling session that evening at home, Philippa couldn't remember the precise moment when the information she sought had been handed to her. She supposed that the social worker must have said something: "Here, then, are the facts you are seeking" was surely too pretentious and theatrical for Miss Henderson's detached professionalism. But some words must have been said, or had she merely taken the General Registrar Office paper from the file and passed it over in silence?

But here it was at last in her hands. She stared at it in disbelief, her first thought that there had been some bureaucratic muddle. There were two names, not one, on the form. Her natural parents were shown as Mary Ducton and Martin John Ducton. She muttered the words to herself. The names meant nothing to her, stirred no memory, evoked no sense of completeness, of forgotten knowledge resurrected at a word to be recognized and acknowledged. And then she saw what must have happened.

She said, hardly realizing that she spoke aloud, "I suppose they married my mother off when they found out that she was pregnant. Probably to a fellow servant. They must have been making that kind of tactful arrangement for generations at Pennington. But I hadn't realized that I was placed for adoption before my mother died. She must have known that she hadn't long to live and wanted to be sure that I would be all right. And, of course, if she were married before I was born the husband would be registered as my father. Nominally I suppose I'm legitimate. It's helpful that she did have a husband. Martin Ducton must have been told that she was pregnant before he agreed to the marriage. She may even have told him before she died

(18)

who my real father was. Obviously the next step is to trace Martin Ducton."

She picked up her shoulder bag and held out her hand to say good-bye. She only half heard Miss Henderson's closing words, the offer of any future help she could give, reiterated advice that Philippa discuss her plans with her adoptive parents, the gently urged suggestion that if she were able to trace her father it should be done through an intermediary. But some words did penetrate her consciousness.

"We all need our fantasies in order to live. Sometimes relinquishing them can be extraordinarily painful, not a rebirth into something exciting and new, but a kind of death."

They shook hands, and Philippa, looking into her face for the first time with any real interest, seeing her for the first time as a woman, detected there a fleeting look which, had she not known better, she might have mistaken for pity.

2

SHE posted her application and check to the Registrar General that evening, 4 July 1978, enclosing, as she had done previously, a stamped addressed envelope. Neither Maurice nor Hilda was curious about her private correspondence, but she didn't want to risk an officially labeled reply falling through the letter box. She spent the next few days in a state of controlled excitement which, for most of the time, drove her out of the house, afraid that Hilda might wonder at her restlessness. Pacing round the lake in St. James's Park, hands deep in her jacket pockets, she calculated when the birth certificate might arrive. Government departments were notoriously slow, but surely this was a simple enough matter. They had only to check their records. And they wouldn't be coping with a rush of applications. The Act had been passed in 1975.

In exactly one week, on Tuesday, 11 July, she saw the familiar envelope on the mat. She took it at once to her own room, calling out to Maurice from the stairs that there was no post for him. She carried it over to the window as if her eyes were growing weaker and she needed more light. The birth certificate, new, crisp, so much more imposing than the shortened form which had served her, as an adopted person, for so long, seemed at first reading to have nothing to do with her. It recorded the birth of a female, Rose Ducton, on 22 May 1960 at 41 Bancroft Gardens, Seven Kings, Essex. The father was shown as Martin John Ducton, clerk; the mother as Mary Ducton, housewife.

So they had left Pennington before she was born. That, perhaps, wasn't surprising. What was unexpected was that they should have moved so far from Wiltshire. Perhaps they had wanted to cut themselves off entirely from the old life, from the gossip, from memories. Perhaps someone had found him a job in Essex, or he might have been returning to his home county. She wondered what he was like, this spurious, accommodating father, whether he had been kind to her mother. She hoped that she could like or at least respect him. He might still live at 41 Bancroft Gardens, perhaps with a second wife and a child of his own. Eighteen years wasn't such a long time. She used the telephone extension in her room to ring Liverpool Street Station. Seven Kings was on the eastern suburban line and in the rush hour there were trains every ten minutes. She left without waiting for breakfast. If there were time, she would get coffee at the station.

The 9:25 train from Liverpool Street was almost empty. It was still early enough for Philippa to be traveling against the commuter tide. She sat in her corner seat, her eyes moving from side to side as the train racketed through the urban sprawl of the eastern suburbs; rows of drab houses with blackened bricks and patched roofs from which sprang a tangle of television aerials, frail crooked fetishes against the evil eye; layered high-rise flats smudged in a distant drizzle of rain; a yard piled high with the glitter of smashed cars in symbolic proximity to the regimented crosses of a suburban graveyard; a paint factory; a cluster of gasometers, pyramids of grit and coal piled beside the track; wastelands rank with weeds; a sloping green bank rising to suburban gardens with their washing lines and toolsheds and children's swings among the roses and hollyhocks. The eastern suburbs, so euphoniously but inappropriately named Maryland, Forest Gate, Manor Park, were alien territory to her, as unvisited and remote from the preoccupations of the last ten years as were the outer suburbs of Glasgow and New York. None of her school friends lived east of Bethnal Green, although a number, unvisited, were reputed to have houses in the few unspoiled Georgian squares off the Whitechapel Road, self-conscious enclaves of culture and radical chic among the tower blocks and the industrial wasteland. Yet the grimy, unplanned urban clutter through which the train rocked and clattered struck some dormant memory, was familiar even in its strangeness, unique despite its bleak uniformity. Surely it wasn't because she had been this way before. Perhaps it was just that the scenery flashing by was so predictably dreary, so typical of the gray purlieus of any large city, that forgotten descriptions, old pictures, and newsprint, snatches of film jumbled in her imagination to produce this sense of recognition. Perhaps everyone had been here before. This drab no-man's land was part of everyone's mental topography.

There were no taxis at Seven Kings Station. She asked the ticket collector the way to Bancroft Gardens. He directed her down the High Street, left down Church Lane, then first on the right. The High Street ran between the railway and the shopping arcade of small businesses with flats above, a launderette, a news agent, a greengrocer, and a supermarket with shoppers already queuing at the checkouts.

There was one scene so vividly recalled, validated by smell and sound and remembered pain that it was impossible to believe she had imagined. A woman wheeling a baby in a pram down just such a street. Herself, little more than a toddler, half stumbling beside the pram, clutching at the handle. The square paving stones speckled with light, unrolling beneath the whirling pram wheels, faster and faster. Her warm grip slipping on the moist metal and the desperate fear that she would lose hold, would be left behind, trampled and kicked under the wheels of the bright red buses. Then a shouted curse. The slap stinging her cheek. A jerk which nearly tore her arm from its socket, and the woman's hand fastening her grip once more on the pram handle. She had called the woman auntie. Auntie May. How extraordinary that she should remember the name now. And the child in the pram had worn a red woolly cap. Its face had been smeared with mucus and chocolate. She remembered that she had hated the child. It must have been winter. The street had been a glare of light and there had been a necklace of colored bulbs swinging above the greengrocer's stall. The woman had stopped to buy fish. She remembered the slab, bright with red-eyed herrings shedding their glistening scales, the strong oleaginous smell of kippers. It could have been this street, only there was no fishmonger here now. She looked down at the paving stones, mottled with rain. Were these the ones over which she had stumbled so desperately? Or was this street, like the terrain each side of the railway, only one more scene from an imagined past?

Turning from the High Street into Church Lane was stepping from drab commercial suburbia into leafy privacy and cosy domesticity. The narrow street, its verge planted with plane trees, curved gently. Perhaps centuries earlier it had indeed been a lane leading to an ancient village church, a building long since demolished or destroyed by bombing in the Second War. All she could see now was a distant stunted spire which looked as if it had been fabricated from slabs of synthetic stone, and topped by a weathervane instead of a cross because of some understandable confusion about the building's function.

And here at last was Bancroft Gardens. Stretching out of sight on either side of the road were identical semidetached houses, each with a path running down the side. They might, she thought, be architecturally undistinguished, but at least they were on a human scale. The gates and railings had been removed and the front gardens were bounded with low bricks walls. The front bay windows were square and turreted, a long vista of ramparted respectability. But the uniformity of the architecture was broken by the individuality of the residents. Every front garden was different, a riot of massed summer flowers, squares of lawn meticulously cut and shaped, stone slabs set about with urns bearing geraniums and ivy.

When Philippa reached number 41 she stopped, amazed. The house stood out from its neighbors by a garish celebration of eccentric taste. The gray London bricks had been painted a shiny red outlined with white pointing. It looked like a house built with immense toy bricks. The crenellations of the bay were alternately red and blue. The window was curtained with net looped across and caught up with satin bows. The original front door had been replaced by one with an opaque glass panel and was painted bright yellow. In the front patch of garden an artificial pond of glass was surrounded by synthetic rocks, on which three gnomes with expressions of grinning imbecility were perched with fishing rods.

As soon as she had pressed the doorbell—it let out a musical jingle—Philippa sensed that the house was empty. The owners were probably at work. She tried once more, but there was no reply. Resisting the temptation to peer through the letter box, she decided to try next door. At least they would know whether Ducton still lived at 41 or where he had gone. The house had no bell and the thud of the knocker sounded unnaturally loud and peremptory. There was no reply. She waited a full minute and was lifting her hand again when she heard the shuffle of feet. The door was opened on a chain, and she glimpsed an elderly woman in apron and hairnet who gave her the unwelcoming suspicious stare of someone to whom no morning visitor at the front door bodes other than ill. Philippa said, "I'm sorry to disturb you, but I wonder if you can help me. I'm looking for a Mr. Martin Ducton who lived next door eighteen years ago. There isn't anyone at home there and I thought you might be able to help."

The woman said nothing, but stood transfixed, one brown clawlike hand still on the door chain, the only visible eye staring blankly at Philippa's face. Then there were more steps, firmer and heavier but still muffled. A male voice said, "Who is it, Ma? What's up?"

"It's a girl, she's asking for Martin Ducton."

The woman's voice was a whisper, sibilant with wonder and a kind of outrage. A chubby male hand released the chain, and the woman stood there, dwarfed by her son. He was wearing slacks topped with a singlet. On his feet were red carpet slippers. Perhaps, thought Philippa, he was a bus driver or conductor relaxing on his rest day. It hadn't been a good time to call. She said apologetically, "I'm sorry to trouble you, but I'm trying to trace a Mr. Martin Ducton. He used to live next door. I wondered whether you might know what happened to him."

"Ducton? He's dead, isn't he? Been dead best part of nine years. Died in Wandsworth Prison."

"In prison?"

"Where else would he be, fucking murderer? He raped that kid, and then he and his missus strangled her. What's he to do with you then? You a reporter or something?"

"Nothing. Nothing. It must be the wrong Ducton. Perhaps I've mistaken the name."

"Someone been having you on more likely. Ducton he was. Martin Ducton. And she was Mary Ducton. Still is."

"She's alive then?"

(24)

"As far as I know. Coming out soon, I shouldn't wonder. Must've done near ten years by now. Not that she'll be coming back next door. Four families have had that place since the Ductons. It always goes cheap, that house. Young couple bought it six months ago. It's not everyone fancies a place where a kid's been done in. Upstairs in the front room it was."

He nodded his head toward number 41, but his eyes never met Philippa's face.

The woman said suddenly, "They should've been hung."

Philippa, astonished, heard herself reply, "Hanged. The word is hanged. They should have been hanged."

"That's right," said the man.

He turned to his mother.

"Buried the kid in Epping Forest, didn't they? Isn't that what they did with her, Ma? Buried her in Epping Forest. Twelve years old she was. You remember, Ma?"

Perhaps the woman was deaf. His last words were an impatient shout. She didn't answer. Still staring at Philippa, she said, "Her name was Julie Scase. I remember now. They killed Julie Scase. But they never got as far as the forest. Caught with the kid's body in the car boot they was. Julie Scase."

Philippa made herself ask through lips so stiff that she could hardly form the words, "Did they have any children? Did you know them?"

"No. We weren't here then. We moved here from Romford after they were inside. There was talk of a kid, a girl, weren't it, who was adopted. Best thing for the poor little bugger."

Philippa said, "Then it's not the same Ducton. This Ducton had no children. I've been given the wrong address. I'm sorry to have troubled you."

She walked away from them down the road. Her legs felt swollen and heavy, weighted bolsters which had no connection with the rest of her body, yet which carried her forward. She looked down at the paving stones, using them as a guide like a drunkard under test. She guessed that the woman and her son were still watching her, and when she had gone about twenty yards she made herself turn round and gaze back at them stolidly. Immediately they disappeared.

Alone now in the empty road, no longer under surveillance, she found that she couldn't go on. She stretched her hands toward the brick wall bordering the nearest garden, found it, and sat. She felt faint and a little sick, her heart constricted like a hot, pulsating ball. But she mustn't faint here, not in this street. Somehow she must get back to the station. She let her head drop between her knees and felt the blood pound back into her forehead. The faintness passed, but the nausea was worse. She sat up again, shutting her eyes against the reeling houses, taking deep gulps of the flower-scented air. Then she opened her eyes and made herself concentrate on the things she could touch and feel. She ran her fingers over the roughness of the wall. Once it had been topped with iron railings. She could feel the coarse grain of the cement-filled holes where they had pierced the brickwork. Perhaps the railings had been taken away in the war to be melted down for armaments. She gazed fixedly at the paving stone under her feet. It was pricked with light, set with infinitesimal specks, bright as diamonds. Pollen from the gardens had blown over it and there was a single flattened rose petal like a drop of blood. How extraordinary that a paving stone should be so varied, should reveal under the intensity of her gaze such gleaming wonders. These things at least were real, and she was real—more vulnerable, less durable than bricks and stones, but still present, visible, an identity. If people passed, surely they would be able to see her.

A youngish woman came out of the house two doors down and walked toward her, pushing a pram with an older child trotting beside it and holding on to the handle. The woman glanced at Philippa, but the child dragged his steps, then turned and gazed back at her with a wide, incurious gaze. He had let go of the pram handle and she found herself struggling to her feet, holding out her arms toward him in warning or entreaty. Then the mother stopped and called to him and the child ran up to her and grasped the pram again.

She watched them until they turned the corner into the High Street. It was time to go. She couldn't sit here all day fastened to the wall as if it were a refuge, the one solid reality in a shifting world. Some words of Bunyan came into her mind and she found herself speaking them aloud: "Some also have wished that the next way to their father's house were here, and that they might be troubled no more with either hills or mountains to go over, but the way is the way, and there is an end."

She didn't know why the words comforted her. She wasn't particularly fond of Bunyan, and she couldn't see why the passage should speak to her confused mind in which disappointment, anguish, and fear struggled for mastery. But as she walked back to the station she spoke the passage over and over again as if the words were in their own way as immutable and solid as the pavement on which she trod. "The way is the way, and there is an end."

3

WHEN he was working, and that was most of the year, Maurice Palfrey used his room at college. The sociology department had swelled since his appointment as senior lecturer, borne on the sixties' tide of optimism and secular faith, and had overflown into an agreeable late eighteenth-century house owned by the college in a Bloomsbury square. He shared the house with the Department of Oriental Studies, colleagues notable for their unobtrusiveness and for the number of their visitors. A succession of small, dark, spectacled men and saried women slid daily through the front door and disappeared into an uncanny silence. He seemed always to be encountering them on the narrow stairs; there were steppings back, bowings, slant-eyed smiles; but only an occasional footfall creaked the upper floor. He felt the house to be infected with secret, micelike busyness.

His room had once been part of the elegant first-floor drawing room, its three tall windows and wrought-iron balcony overlooking the square gardens, but it had been divided to provide a room for his secretary. The grace of the proportions had been destroyed and the delicately carved overmantel, the George Morland oil which had always hung in the business room at Pennington and which he had placed above it, the two Regency chairs looked pretentious and spurious. He felt the need to explain to visitors that he hadn't furnished his room with reproductions. And the conversion hadn't been a success. His secretary had to pass through his room to get to hers, and the clatter of the typewriter through the thin partition was so irritating a metallic *obbligato* to his meetings that he had to tell Molly to stop working when he had visitors. It was difficult to concentrate during meetings when he was aware that she was sitting next door glowering across her machine in sullen, ostentatious idleness. Elegance and beauty had been sacrificed for a utility which wasn't even efficient. Helena, on her first visit to the room, had merely said, "I don't like conversions" and hadn't visited again. Hilda, who hadn't appeared to notice or care about the room's proportions, had left the department after their marriage and had never come back.

The habit of working away from home had begun after his marriage to Helena when she had bought 68 Caldecote Terrace. Walking hand in hand through the empty, echoing rooms like exploring children, folding back the shutters so that the sun came through in great shafts and lay in pools on the unpolished boards, the pattern of their future together had been laid down. She had made it plain that there would be no intrusion